TARMAC AND SCRAP

AND OTHER CORNISH TALES

BY **ELIZABETH ALWAY**

GW00806427

TRAFFORD
PUBLISHING

USA • Canada • UK • Ireland

© Copyright 2006 Carol Elizabeth Alway Ring.

Note for Librarians: a cataloguing record for this book that includes Dewey Decimal
Classification and US Library of Congress numbers is available from the Library and Archives
of Canada. The complete cataloguing record can be obtained from their online database at:
www.collectionscanada.ca/amicus/index-e.html
ISBN 1-4120-9516-6

Printed in Victoria, BC, Canada

Printed on paper with minimum 30% recycled fibre.

Trafford's print shop runs on "green energy" from solar, wind and other environmentally-friendly power sources.
Offices in Canada, USA, Ireland and UK
This book was published *on-demand* in cooperation with Trafford Publishing. On-demand
publishing is a unique process and service of making a book available for retail sale to the
public taking advantage of on-demand manufacturing and Internet marketing. On-demand
publishing includes promotions, retail sales, manufacturing, order fulfilment, accounting and
collecting royalties on behalf of the author.

Book sales for North America and international:
Trafford Publishing, 6E–2333 Government St.,
Victoria, BC v8t 4p4 CANADA
phone 250 383 6864 (toll-free 1 888 232 4444)
fax 250 383 6804; email to orders@trafford.com
Book sales in Europe:
Trafford Publishing (uk) Limited, 9 Park End Street, 2nd Floor
Oxford, UK OX1 1HH UNITED KINGDOM
phone 44 (0)1865 722 113 (local rate 0845 230 9601)
facsimile 44 (0)1865 722 868; info.uk@trafford.com
Order online at:
trafford.com/06-1271

10 9 8 7 6 5 4 3

Contents

One

Mrs. Tregaskis

Dr. and Mrs. Tregaskis retired to his native Cornwall after a not-unsuccessful career abroad. Dr. Tregaskis's success was far from undeserved; though not brilliant, he was more than competent, and conscientious and discreet in the application of his Hippocratic oath. His one true gift was his ability to see the best in others, without envy or bias, while not being blind to their faults. His was rather like an intelligent and loyal canine nature; the gundog roused by master staggering drunk, who opens one eye and goes back to sleep, ready to offer him affection in the morning when he's sober. Dr. Tregaskis was not loved for nothing by his friends and patients.

Mrs. Tregaskis's nature was different. She wasn't a "typical doctor's wife"—she was too witty, regal, good-looking in her youth, and had had a high opinion of her due. Like many women of her class and time, serious work was unnecessary, and abroad she had had nannies and servants; she had confined her considerable abilities to social and sartorial matters. She arranged excellent dinner parties and looked and behaved the perfect hostess; she flirted a little but whether her indiscretions were ever major no one really knew. Only those friends, whose upheavals left them so upset they forgot they were a little afraid of her, discovered her warm and generous heart in private; so she too was the object of loyal affection in some quarters. This big-heartedness eventually came to her rescue, though in an unexpected manner.

Back in Cornwall, when consoled against the damp by a couple of old-fashioned cocktails, Mrs. Tregaskis bewailed her lost position and beauty from a safe distance. She had drunk relatively little abroad, for sun and alcohol are renowned ruiners of complexion, but Mrs. Tregaskis's drinking of cocktails at six progressed to gin at three. Having hit on the felicitous excuse of the Cornish weather for her change in habits, she was rarely without a reason. Dr. Tregaskis observed this change and took to surreptitiously watering the gin. Eventually Mrs. Tregaskis opined that, like everything else, gin wasn't what it had been; and he held his hand, lest his wife remember Polish spirit.

They were well enough liked in the Cornish village, where they had retired to an over-large house, purchased years before as an insurance. Dr. Tregaskis occasionally did locum work, and his kind manner and air of professional solicitude assured him his supporters; and his adequate pension meant he could pay properly, in that economically-depressed county, for gardening, odd jobs, and logs, and this made him more welcome. They were both tall, and this tallness impressed the older Cornish, and helped confirm their position as a class apart, almost gentry. This latter classification gratified Mrs. Tregaskis, and made the Cornish wives more comfortable when they met her obviously tipsy; for everyone knows there is an honourable tradition of eccentric English gentlewomen. The land behind their house looked out on moorland, with a distant view of the sea.

A further stretch of this moorland was the site of one of Cornwall's biggest china clay pits, which had steadily eaten into the surrounding hillsides. In the years since the purchase of the house, the white clean hills of clay waste crept nearer until only their own large shelter belt of ancient Monterey pines, five acres away, seemed to hold back the advance of Cornwall's one successful heavy industry. Powerless to force a sale, the china clay company tried to tempt one with ever-increasing offers that arrived with despairing regularity. It was a great comfort to Dr. and Mrs. Tregaskis that they owned all the mineral and other rights to their acreage. This had not been so with the several small moorland farms that had disappeared in the last twenty years, although their adequately compensated owners often cared little. Mrs. Tregaskis, who was far from unaware when it came to divining the feelings behind outward social niceties, suspected several of the village wives with sons or husbands unemployed regretted her grounds standing between them and the advance of the clay works. But for her, the romantic gnarled and kingly pines, with a glimpse of shining sea between their branches, came to represent a bastion against ugliness, change, and ensuing chaos. Although everything seemed so settled, and every likely eventuality catered for, in the lives of Dr. and Mrs. Tregaskis, change, even upheaval, was just around the corner.

The change originated in the most unlikely spot. It started with the disquiet the old-fashioned Dr. Tregaskis felt when he tried to grapple with the confusion the world around him caused his conscientious soul. He did occasional work as a locum, for an elderly practitioner in the health centre in the poorest part of the nearest town. Then, he found himself face to face with a world he felt as unfamiliar with as he had with the Africa he met when he first went out; only then he had been young, and learning had been easier. He looked around in vain for signs of reverence of values he had always held dear, for family pride and marital stability, for respect and seemliness. There had been unarguable material advances, but poor Dr. Tregaskis could only see the negative side of the social changes.

Unexpectedly, he was asked, one summer, to stand in for six weeks; with some misgivings, he agreed. The six weeks became a burden; he had great difficulty in believing he was breaking no law when he prescribed contraception for a confident, cheeky sixteen-year-old. The blasé cynicism he sometimes met appalled him. Dr. Tregaskis's true gift, of seeing the best in unpromising cases, became exhausted, working in unfamiliar ground and unaccustomedly hard. He tried to open his heart to his wife, but she had always poured a gin by the time surgery closed, and all she would say was how right he was, the quality of the world had dived in recent years. Mrs. Tregaskis, who would have helped if she could, knew too little of the world around her now to be of much aid to him. One evening in warm July, his thoughts weighing on his mind, remembering to whistle the surprised dog, Dr. Tregaskis set out on foot for the local public house in the village a mile or two away. It was a pleasant walk and a pleasant evening; enough of the patrons knew him for him to feel at ease; and good English beer, after so many cocktails, was a rediscovered joy. He took to going several times a week, never drinking much. Mrs. Tregaskis encouraged him. Behind the bar in the "Rising Sun," worked part-time a widowed woman in her fifties, busy, kind, and trim: Mrs. Williams. One day she arrived in his surgery with a sickly child of nearly three, and in the ensuing crisis that a diagnosis of whooping cough started, Dr. Tregaskis saw much of her. It turned out the child was not a daughter's but her youngest son's by a teenage girlfriend. Since almost birth the child had been cared for by his grandmother, and he and she loved each other. Mrs. Williams's legal fostering of the child became a cause they both believed in. The natural parents were approached, the legal necessities considered. A bit shame-faced, the son accepted it; it was an easy solution for him. Brazenly the ex-girlfriend wished them well of it; she was off, quite free now. Dr. Tregaskis remembered checking the files and finding with some relief that Mrs. Williams herself was not a patient; people might misconstrue their friendship. Mrs. Tregaskis teased Dr. Tregaskis over his attachment to the case; but secretly she didn't mind at all. It was good for him to do something he believed in, and she had discovered a new friend in the gardener, who encouraged her interest in her garden, and far from disapproving of her drinking, would take a glass with her. She explained African beliefs in tree spirits; sometimes, when the sun was setting behind her pines, it seemed it must be just so; and the gardener liked her tales as well.

However, Dr. Tregaskis's friendship outstripped that of Mrs. Tregaskis, and passed over that bar that divides, for most of us, the ordinary social world of friends from the magic-tinged, booby-trapped mountainous landscape of the heart. Mrs. Tregaskis, who could sometimes hear more than that which was just said, divined this almost before her husband. In truth she told herself, she had little to be jealous of; she was, although a decade older, the handsomer of the pair, and richer, more worldly wise, sophisticated. All of this was true.

To make sure she would not be laughed at, she told her gardener friend of her husband's "peccadillo," so at least the villagers would know she knew, and know she brushed it off. She refused to look into the future; she took refuge in the past, remembered some escapades with dashing men. She was no fool, she knew she had been the object of illicit desire, not love, and as time wore on, she knew that love must be what Mrs. Williams and Dr. Tregaskis offered one another. Sometimes she cried, out of loneliness and pique. Dr. Tregaskis did not love her now. She took to talking to the dog about what she should do, as she strolled in her five acres. He was getting old; she wondered if it would be wise to get a pup, and whether he would take more kindly to a female one. At regular intervals the china clay company wrote to them; their five acres inconvenienced more and more operations, she inferred. Mrs. Tregaskis wondered when the next offer would arrive. She was now, without quite realizing it, beginning to make plans.

Poor Dr. Tregaskis, who lived in a world of moral absolutes

where he himself was concerned, however tolerant he might be of others' foibles, suffered weeks of torment. Eventually, he asked Mrs. Tregaskis for a divorce. Mrs. Tregaskis dissolved in tears, and Dr. Tregaskis's torment heightened. He had already found himself, shame-facedly, weighing what he would lose with what he would gain; and most of all, after being made to feel the cad he felt he must be, he dreaded living penned in by Mrs. William's neighbours in the village. Mrs. Tregaskis drove home both points with the benefit of a lifetime-marriage's practice. She railed and recriminated, wept and swore, drank, slept, woke, and railed again. They had been married thirty years; she had borne his children, she had refused offers from prestigious men to stand by him as a young doctor abroad; was this to be her reward, abandonment for a Cornish barmaid? Well, barwoman. Had she kept it up, it is doubtful Dr. Tregaskis could have left her. But Mrs. Tregaskis was not just a vain and stylish woman; she knew she gave her husband very little nowadays; she admitted to herself she did not miss him much when he wasn't there. Deep down, she felt it was not fair to stop him, just because the fear of loneliness sometimes gripped and terrified her. Once she had convinced herself she could keep him if she really wanted, she held her head high and told him he could have his divorce.

So they resolved their affairs: a separation ensued, followed by a divorce by mutual consent. Mrs. Tregaskis interviewed the chief accountant of the china clay company, and achieved a price for "The Gables" that staggered and impressed the locals, and ensured comfort all round: a home and pension for her, and the wherewithal for a more dignified nest for Dr. Tregaskis and Mrs. Williams, and of course the "grandson." Having made certain that the trees would inevitably be felled, Mrs. Tregaskis had made it a condition of the sale that the belt of giant pines be cut down within a certain week, and that week she took a taxi to the station and visited an old friend in Hastings.

When her friend in Hastings asked her, over gin and angostura bitters, why she was being so bloody reasonable, she replied that she couldn't have poor Edgar living cheek-by-jowl with all his new wife's neighbours, his heart would never stand it. Her friend remembered her reputation for irony and wit, and smiled to see it had not deserted her.

On her return, Mrs. Tregaskis bought a Dalmatian bitch puppy. She had purchased an undoubtedly pretty cottage — no cottage at all really, rather a small manor house, with tiny-paned stone mullion windows and an ancient, huge, and healthy wisteria. It stood in the church town, near the parish church, away from the village and out of sight of her old property.

She and the gardener set to work perfecting nature's handiwork, and the garden became locally famous. It was opened to the public in aid of charity, and was much admired. Equally importantly, this led to a new circle of friends among older people who loved plants and cared very little if a person's appearance wasn't chic. Mrs. Tregaskis slowly relaxed; she forgot to colour her hair, and let it grow and put it up into a chignon. When the old dog from Africa died, she bought another puppy, a Labrador this time. Her children always stayed with her, partly out of loyalty to the parent on her own, and partly because it was so much easier to impose their own small children on their mother, than on Dr. Tregaskis's new house-hold. So things settled down, and a couple of years went by.

Mrs. Tregaskis had settled down in her new, different life. Dr. Tregaskis and his second wife continued in contentment. After a pressing couple of days as a locum in town, the doctor was return-ing home one early evening when, caught in the heat of a holiday makers' traffic jam, he suffered a stroke. He lived on for a month, utterly confused now as to his true marital state, and even the iden-tity of his wives. His constant chatter, largely unintelligible to Mrs. Williams (as she had been), was nevertheless plainly of Africa, and she knew he was not reassuring her that she was still the toast of Nairobi. Gingerly, she telephoned Mrs. Tregaskis.

A summons to what was after all a deathbed could not be ig-nored. Mrs. Tregaskis put on her gold and amber earrings, checked her reflection in the mirror, and set out down the half-dozen miles of lane in her new little car.

Over the next few weeks, these visits became a daily habit. Mrs. Tregaskis and her successor, with the cause of any past contention fading before their eyes, got on well enough. After Dr. Tregaskis died, in the local hospital, the two widows, as the Cornish called them, attended the funeral in the local church with dignity, managing to appear, if not united in grief, then at least in genuine sadness. Unseemly melodrama was avoided.

At Churchtown Manor, things went on as before. Mrs. Tregaskis, freed from any remnant of nagging heartache now her husband was dead, enjoyed her dogs, her garden, and the friendship of her gardener—whom she increasingly employed—and his extensive family. When she got depressed, she went on a binge, then slept it off. This didn't happen often, and the children visited. When she was on her own, it gave Mrs. Tregaskis a warm and rosy feeling to remember that her farmer neighbours answered, when asked by visitors, who lived in that amazingly beautiful cottage and garden? "Mrs. Tregaskis. Dr. Tregaskis (God rest him) runned off with a woman from round 'ere when he was old enough to know better; but Mrs. Tregaskis, now, she's a real lady." She would sit by the fire with a gin, and reflect that this was a more fitting title at her age, than the ex-belle of Nairobi.

Two

The Steeplechase and
Mary Hawker

The shiny dark green landrover turned into the car park of the Ring
O'Bells, pulling a new double horsebox, and parked. Two gleaming
thoroughbred rear ends stamped bossily in the box, while the two
women, ignoring the horses' impatience to be home, walked into
the pub. Both were above average in size, strong and big but not
fat: the younger one had thick glossy black hair, the elder a strong
jaw and grizzled brown hair.

"Is that the local lady of the manor and her hunters?" asked
the visitor, sitting outside in the early March sunshine despite the
chilly wind. "Not quite!" said old Fred the potman. "That's Mary
Hawker that was, and Ginny Sullivan, her girl."

Mary Hawker was born nearly sixty years ago on a small moorland farm out near Polmenna. The moorland had first been 'taken in' back in the 1840's when the local landowners had encouraged tenants to break moorland, and the tiny low granite house and yard buildings dated from then. For two generations livings were made and families were raised; for one generation people struggled; and by Mary's birth, the farms were so out-of-date agriculturally they were sold off cheap to the sitting tenants. One day subsidies would increase their worth, but not enough; and so Mary was born into a bullock-rearing, muscovy-ducks-in-the-yard farming family with old-fashioned skills, limited opportunities, and a hunger for making money. She was one of three girls, and all of them could ride the unshod and half-broken moorland ponies over anything. Mary was the best, because the most fearless. Both her sisters married; one a local farmer, a younger version of their father, the other a charming handsome dipsomaniac with a racehorse. Mary left school when she could; and helped out on the farm. She rode at every opportunity, and bought herself a bigger, better horse than she had been used to.

Still unmarried, a local phenomenon gave her her chance. Eventually closed down by officials, for over a decade pony racing enjoyed a vogue in North Cornwall. For eight weeks in the summer, weekly races were held on a farm near the coast on big flat fields overlooking the sea. There was a beer tent, and bookies attended and set up their booths. The holidaymakers from the coastal caravan parks and campsites came too, and their lack of horse sense and the consumption of lager and the holiday atmosphere made their gentle fleecing easy by the canny Cornish pony runners. The smaller ponies were ridden by children, but the bigger ones by adults, and the wildest ones by Mary. It is harder to stop a fired-up pony running than anyone who hasn't tried it can imagine; but Mary usually could. On a proper racecourse she would have been stopped, but pulling a favourite usually went unnoticed here, and thus the bets were fixed, by the owners and riders, enough to make money but not enough to anger the bookies to the point where they refused to attend.

So, by trading the risk of broken bones, Mary made some money, and grew in fearlessness, and in time moved on to better things. As beef subsidies grew steadily one of the area's moor farmers in particular invested his surplus in thoroughbred steeplechasers, who ran, and sometimes won, in the hunt point-to-points, all over the region from Exeter westwards. To qualify, the horses had to be hunted a number of times with the appropriate hunt; Mary rode for Ben Sobey, and her fearlessness, and firmness with the recalcitrant, grew greater. She was thirty-seven, and still unmarried.

At this time the old main road down Cornwall's spine was being dualled—turned into an almost-motorway. It began in the east, and crept, with its culture-changing menace, down the county. With the road works came the Irish, and with the Irish came Patsy Sullivan. It has often been remarked that Eire and Cornwall have things in common and perhaps they do. Despite his unusual nickname, Patrick Sullivan was a hard man, born on a small farm in the far west of Ireland, used to handling heavy horses as a boy, driven to England by poverty and used now to driving heavy machinery, with a brogue to match Mary's Cornish dialect, and at forty-one tired of picking up pub women, and ready to settle down, though he didn't quite realize it himself yet.

The Irish, who were staying temporarily in the Ring O'Bells, started going to the pony races. They enjoyed the drinking and betting and the proximity of horses. Patsy had seen Mary before, but never on a horse; he was impressed. Rather shy if he hadn't had a few beers, he said he would bet on her pony. She looked at him sideways, then came to a decision and leant down and muttered, "Not on this one." The pony lost, and a friendly complicity started between them.

A few weeks later, Mary was sitting on a bar stool, with her mother beside her, unusually in the pub, and unusually in a skirt. Patsy and the boys came in, greeted, and moved along. A local

20

nuisance, a big strong farmer who could not hold his drink, and a famous groper, came in, on sufferance, and an air of expectancy ran round the local patrons who knew his reputation. He approached Mary and muttered. "Bugger off, Des," said Mary. He maundered on, "Don't be like that," and lurched. His hand was on her thigh; he ran it upwards. Mary swung her right hand, still perched on her stool, and cracked him on the jaw, and he crumpled. He lay there, out cold. The bar guffawed. "Christ Mary, I wouldn't fall out with you. Proper old nuisance, Des," said the landlord. Patsy stood up, walked over, picked up Des's collar, and dragged him, still prone, outside, and left him there. "Let me buy you a drink," he said to Mary and her mother. And so a romance, only unlikely on the surface, began. It ran through the summer and into the autumn, and survived Christmas, that testing time. Patsy went back to Eire briefly, the road moved on, the steeple-chasing season began again, and still Patrick and Mary were going about together. At a big meeting, run by the smart hunt near Exeter, Mary won the open, on Bill Sobey's chestnut gelding.

For Mary, this was a high point, a ne plus ultra of ambition, an achievement she had thought she would only ever dream of. She was congratulated by people in burberrys, whose accents were so correct she could hardly understand them; Ben Sobey swaggered and beamed, and made a bit of a fool of himself, aping the gentry as his stable boy and driver muttered to each other. But they soon returned home, driving swiftly down the improved dual carriage-way Patsy had helped lay. After the horses had been seen to, they burst furious with pride and excitement into the Ring O'Bells for the real celebration, with those who mattered, those who knew them, where they had all started from (for Ben's start was as hum-ble as Mary's). People came in as the news spread; the Irish boys, who had been at the races, had got home first and were already merry, Patsy among them. The evening wore on, the atmosphere got louder and more raucous as drink was poured, smoke billowed, shorts of whisky and gin followed: finally Ben bought champagne (which no-body was much used to, but it seemed the thing to do). Mary drank champagne from the cup the horse she had ridden had won, and felt herself in heaven. Patsy proposed a toast to horse and rider and owner, and then, full of pride, and a bit of possessiveness, he proposed.

He wondered afterward, although he never regretted it, if he had done it in public so he couldn't go back on it, or if he just needed to be drunk to have the courage, and was showing off a bit. He asked Mary to marry him; she didn't reply. She gaped, and he said firmly "You'll give up the racing now. Not the horses, but the racing. It's not safe for women, especially if they're breeding." Mary burst into tears, and hit him, but he didn't much notice. "You bastard!" she yelled, and the pub, taking this as acceptance, drank the couple's health, several times.

They did marry. They surprised themselves by feeling very happy, once the deed was done. Patsy bought a bungalow with some land and put up a couple of stables, and about a year later Virginia was born, looking exactly like her father and mother's daughter, and named for the Virgin Mary. They stayed happy enough, and prospered in a small way, and followed the racing avidly, and dealt a little in horses, always advantageously. Ginny lapsed from the faith when she left school, but Patsy still (usually) went to Mass on Sundays, and to the pub straight after. Mary and Patsy had rescued each other from a future of lonely singledom and childlessness; and she never did ride in a race again.

And that, to answer the question asked of Fred the potman that started this tale, is the story of Mary Hawker that was. It is of an energetic life, intensely lived, with an outcome as successful and happy as most would settle for, but definitely not the story of "the local lady of the manor."

Three

Rosewarne Farmhouse

Peter Courtney walked back down the farm track to Rosewarne farmhouse, which he had not long purchased, and breathed a deep sigh of satisfaction.

He had known as a child that his family had come from the west country a couple of generations ago, and this knowledge had warmed him growing up on a suburban estate in a dull Northern town, and stayed with him in London as he slowly made money. It blossomed again, as approaching fifty, he realized he could work, thanks to computers and the internet, and earn, many miles from London, if he chose.

His wife didn't quite share his enthusiasm but was perfectly happy to move to the country in principle: their grown-up son and daughter would probably visit West Penwith more readily than

North Finchley. He was fascinated by the farmhouse: although
it was a late eighteenth century building, he knew the site dated
back to the early Middle Ages. Archaeological opinion placed the
original, squat primitive manor house beneath the bumps above the
stream in the one remaining field that belonged to him. The manor
had become an ordinary farm, and the European Union and modern
strictures, and subsidies, had led to the amalgamation of farms and
the lucrative sale of redundant farmhouses to—well, people like
him. At least he had a deep interest in his location, and was prepared to invest more than money in his new life, he thought.

The sun had set, but it was still light, and a blackbird was
singing somewhere in the tall, sycamore-filled hedge. Suddenly,
breaking the peace, was the noise again: frantic fast hoof beats, like
something out of a cowboy film. The noise gathered, and seemed
to pass him by, and faded towards the road in the western moorland direction. He had heard it a couple of times before in the past
week; he couldn't pin it down but assumed it was a half-wild pony
careering around in a neighbouring field. If he had been more of a
countryman, he would have wondered why the hoof beats didn't
change tone, as the pony seemed to take to the tarmac surface of
the road; but he wasn't, so he didn't.

The next day the local builder was in the kitchen. This room, as
is not uncommon in farmhouses in the far west, was only divided
from the barn next door by a tongue-and-groove partition, that

had plainly been patched, a long time ago, in an inexpert way that Peter thought was rather charming. "You need to scat that down and replace it with a proper block wall," announced Frank. "I'll use thermolite, or all your expensive heat will rush straight through." Peter protested that he rather liked the partition; but Frank was so insistent, and so persuasive about the loss of heat that would occur in the dank months of January and February, that Peter gave in.

The outdoor work he was doing did Peter good, physically and mentally.

Apart from the building work, he was making a vegetable patch, something he never had room or time for in London. There was a huge ancient muck-heap in the yard which had to be moved anyway, and the loamy soil it provided was ideal for his garden. He found all sorts in it; old horse shoes, a couple of bridle bits, and an ancient shotgun. They would all look good on the wall in the kitchen, Peter thought. Things went on in a satisfactory manner. Peter thought he heard the unseen pony once or twice, but it was summertime and people might well gallop about in fields for all he knew, and he paid it no heed.

When Sally came down in June her surprise, and pleasure, pleased him enormously. He needed really to get back to paid work soon, and the elimination of the minor worry that she'd hate it — or just not like it much — was the first step on the way. Their dog, a middle-aged sort of collie, black and white, originally from

Battersea, was in heaven. She loved the field and stream, the walks, lost weight and began to look like a (well-kept) farm dog. She didn't like the barn, and positively hackled up at the builder's new wall, or the area in front of it; but that was all.

Peter's daughter came in July, with a friend who had a toddler: the weather was idyllic, and they picnicked in the field, and the child made daisy chains. One day he wandered into the barn and was found screaming and sobbing shortly afterwards; all he would say was "The man! The man!" and cry. After an understandable panic about would-be abductors, a thorough search was made. The neighbours at the cottage by the turning off the road were asked if they had seen anything. One old man said, awkwardly, it's probably nothing, that old house has funny corners you know; children, dogs, sense things we don't. He wouldn't be drawn further, and Peter began to wonder if Rosewarne had a ghost. He quite liked the idea, if the truth be told; maybe the pony was its charger. His mind began to picture mounted men in mediaeval homespun, the un-Hollywood old gentry as they might have been.

He looked in his deeds and reaffirmed the name of the farmers there, who last seriously farmed, as Creber; there were loads of Crebers about, he'd ask. He first asked, luckily, on his own in the local pub, of the landlord, who advised against asking the family and said they wouldn't welcome that, he didn't think. Also the eldest of the Crebers had died just about the time Peter had bought the farm; it wouldn't be tactful. But there was a garrulous elderly local labourer up at the Miner's Arms, who'd tell a tale to anyone for free beer. He lived in a caravan down a lane up there.

When the summer was over, Peter sought him out and took him to the pub, and settled down to listen.

Well, it was like this, see. Back before subsidies — and this was before the War, farming was in a slump — you could buy up these moorland farms for a song by today's standards, and people did, poor as they were, saved and scrimped, bought land. It meant more, then. Well, you'll have heard tell of the Crebers. There's lots of them in this parish and between them, they own a lot. All of 'em rake in subsidies and suchlike. Well, I expect you've heard Denzil Creber died a couple of months back — huge funeral, farmers always go to each others' funerals even if they didn't much like the dead one. Now the Crebers started where you are now. Their mother married a widow-man from Trecara, and they bought this place of yours — with eighty-odd acres then. She had a few boys, who all live around here — well, apart from Denzil, of course, now — and a girl, who married a man from Falmouth, and left. Good thing, in some ways. Now, Mrs. Creber and her man fought. They say like cat and dog — they were more like a fox and an old badger. Of course, they had those kids, so they must have stopped sometimes, but the rest of the time, they fought. The trouble was, old man Creber had a son and daughter,

29

grown, by his first marriage, down Stithians way, and he would threaten, using them. Well, when Denzil was about seventeen (he was the eldest of the second family) things had got to an awful pitch. After rowing for days, old man Creber announced he was going in to see lawyer Harvey next day and change his will: leave everything to Marcus and Sarah, and bail out, leave. They could live there but they wouldn't ever own it, Mrs. Creber and her boys. No wives' rights like now, then, see. What happened next was never proved but folk know. Old man Creber used to clean his shotgun in the barn, on that bench the other side of the wall from the kitchen. That night, not wanting to be with them I suppose, he sat out there, cleaning, fiddling with his mole traps, and so on. By ten o'clock that evening, Ben Creber was lying on the ground with his head half blown off, and a big hole in the partition. The police came, and treated it with suspicion, but they all told the same story — suicide — and of course the science wasn't like it is today. Denzil was the only one who wasn't there; out on the moor, looking for sheep, got caught by the dark and late back. Of course folk think he was there, and there was an arguement, a struggle, a fight, or some such, and the gun went off. The people in the cottage at the crossroads near your entrance swore they heard a horse going hell for leather out the farm track and up the lane towards the moor, just after half past nine. Of course there was no traffic to speak of then, and the road wasn't tarmacked. So you could've galloped all the way to Galver on a hard pony; and I think Denzil did.

Peter left the pub with his mind racing, and drove, with the sunset behind him, musing how this road had so changed from its beginning as a wandering track, and now carried big 4wds, and cars doing fifty miles an hour. He was too honest not to admit his ownership of Rosewarne farmhouse was part of the same set of changes, but hoped he would be a more neutral presence. As he turned into the welcome quiet of the lane his thoughts turned back to the house.

So it wasn't a mediaeval ghost, then; not at all. He found the story hadn't put him off a bit; and it was quite possibly not true. He remembered the landlord's wry remark of "He'd tell a tale to anyone for free beer." But perhaps he wouldn't tell Sally — he'd just carry on as if he knew no more than he had earlier that evening. Perhaps he'd have that sensitive end of the barn blocked off, to keep dogs and children out, and say if anyone commented, that it was for insulation. He didn't need that much space, after all.

And he'd get rid of that old shotgun he'd dug up. It wouldn't look good to him on the wall, now.

Four

The Quarrel

This is a story of fox-hunting folk: but not quite what you might expect.

Unlike the famous hunts of the midland shires, the hunts west and north of Exeter are often farmers' hunts. By the time Norman Penhaligon got his Mastership, anyone who rode well enough, and was careless enough of personal safety, could usually afford to hunt, and around the moors of Cornwall the open land gives the opportunity of enjoying the kind of wild run across country that made hunting the dare-devil sport that was its original appeal.

Hunts have specific "countries" — areas where, with the permission of the landowners, they can hunt foxes with hounds. High on Bodmin moor, years ago, a pack of harriers was set up, to hunt hares, and since the quarry was different, the harrier pack, known as Wildworks Harriers, had a "country" that was half in the fox-hunting Eglos Hounds' country and half in the Northmoor Hounds' country.

Now that the hares had almost disappeared, the Wildworks too hunted foxes, and this potential use of the same territory by two different packs hunting the same prey provided fertile ground for quarrels to spring up in.

Norman Penhaligon, a farmer, was Master of the Eglos Foxhounds. Norman's first love had been horses, and through his hard childhood on the edge of the moor, and his early manhood on moor farms raising beef bullocks, he had always ridden horses when he could, bought them when he could afford to, and dreamed of them at night. When he married Jean, a neighbour, but an educated daughter of a gentleman farmer originally from up-country, love of horses was really what they had in common. They had had two children, who were grown now and married; it was almost as if they had forgotten them now and reverted to their first, four-legged, loves. Norman had become Master nearly a decade ago; he was popular enough, easy-going and affable, and Jean's background helped by providing any polish he may have lacked. Jean and Norman made a handsome pair when mounted on their grey horses, in red coats, Master and whipper-in, with the hounds milling about at foot.

Norman was easy-going, affable, and lazy. He built kennels at the farm, rather than keep the hounds at the hunt kennels, because it was easier, and saved a full-time kennelman's wages, and the hunt premises needed serious repairs anyway. The sport was better nearer home, the gallops on the moor more fun than working hounds in the enclosed, farming country of the south-east. But those hunt members, who lived in the south-east of Eglos country, complained from time to time about always having to box their horses to meets. The grumbles from that neck of the woods were growing; Norman felt they had a point, and was meaning to do something about it.

Things ran smoothly enough until Jean went off. Jean had gone off, usually with a man, from time to time during their long marriage. Norman consoled himself locally, if he could; Jean always came back, and things went on as before. But this time she went further, and for longer, than usual — a fisherman in West Penwith — and her disappearance made Normal vulnerable to those who were interested in what he had, and who began plotting.

On a farm close to Norman's lived Anne Trelawney, Jean's sister. She was older, less outward-going, than her younger sister, married to Olver, and not at all given to running off. She was far more concerned with the futures of her children. The son was earmarked for their farm, one daughter had married the son of the

Master of Northmoor foxhounds, and the couple worked for him and would probably one day get that farm and the hounds. The second daughter, Maria, had returned from a spell away, married to a young man who had had a post in a posh, up-country hunt, and was staying with his wife's parents. Anne Trelawney was a woman with a son-in-law in need of a job.

Her youngest daughter, Dora, pretty and seventeen, had attracted the attention of McNeill, a blacksmith from south of Hawkstor. He had aspirations to the daughter (and her inheritance to come one day) and maybe to a hunt mastership. No-one but McNeill himself saw him as a serious contender for either, but his ambition meant he could be useful to Anne Trelawney. He single-mindedly stirred up resentment when he could as he travelled round shoeing horses.

Poor Norman, potentially weakened by the latent disaffection his keeping the hounds at home had caused, unthinking of the pitfalls of the shared territory with the Wildworks Harriers, and now enfeebled by Jean's untimely desertion, was looking more and more like ripe prey.

With Jean away, Norman struggled with the social politics necessary for his position at the best of times, and now was far from that. Conscious of the feeling among the south-eastern members of his hunt, and very much aware of a meet scheduled for their part of the country coming up, he thought it would be a good idea to persuade as many of his locals as he could to travel down, so things would look more even, and everyone feel they were treated equally. This wasn't a good idea; for the travellers included the very ones seeking to find fault with him.

The meet wasn't a success; the country, with roads criss-crossing it, properly farmed and too heavily wooded for horses in some places, meant galloping was limited, and worst of all, they couldn't find a fox. Anne Trelawney, with the out-of-work son-in-law, listened apparently in agreement while McNeill complained to everyone who would listen, "Fine way to exercise hounds. But this isn't hunting!"

In the pub later, the son-in-law joined in, making odious comparisons between Norman and the better-run, more professional hunts he had known up-country. Norman Penhaligon felt miserable that night. He sent the lad from the village, who was now both part-time kennelman and whipper-in, home, and fed the hounds himself. At least *they* were grateful. Not one to bear grudges or dwell on his sorrows, he still chafed under the injustice of being compared to other, up-country, hunts, with five times the subscriptions, and five times the money for himself and upkeep of hounds.

Perceiving himself between a rock and hard place, Norman had what he thought was a bright idea. He would shut his local critics up by calling an extra meet, unscheduled, here on the farm—where he knew plenty of foxes flourished in the unkempt fringes—and give them all a hell-for-leather gallop on the moors, and if they broke their necks, so much the better, he thought, with uncharacteristic venom. He forgot what Jean would have remembered, that this corner of the country was also hunted by Wildworks Harriers.

He put an advert in the paper calling the meet in three days' time, pleased he remembered the deadline time. He didn't fancy the pub that night. Probably McNeill would be there, flirting with Dora, and his sister-in-law would be sitting like a spider on the edge of a stretched web. If Jean were here, she'd put them right with a remark and a laugh, but she wasn't. No local consolation had turned up this time. Fishing boats! That was a new one. Farmers, a blacksmith, even a solicitor once, but never before a fisherman.

When he did go to the pub, it was the evening of the day the advert had appeared in the paper. The penny still hadn't dropped. He'd forgotten the Wildworks Harriers' legitimate, scheduled meet two days after his, and on his brother-in-law's farm next door to his. His idea of giving good sport to the complainers meant that afterwards no fox would be in the area for a week, and Wildworks would be cheated of all their sport. He'd successfully provided marvellous ammunition for his enemies, without giving it a thought.

Norman walked into the Plume of Feathers unaware of the volcano about to erupt.

The pub was full, mostly of local folk, but was strangely quiet of the normal hubbub. People sat as if at a performance, and were listening to the deep voice of one man. Olver Trelawney was in the centre of the bar, glaring and beered-up. His family, in-laws, and McNeill sat round, like watchers at a dog-fight, all expectance. "Bloody fool! Has he got no sense, or is he just an idiot? Calling a scratch meet two days before Harriers? What sport will they get? All the foxes gone into Devon? We'll *all* be exercising hounds, not hunting. I'll shut my bloody gates to 'en, I will. No Eglos hounds on my ground on Thursday!"

He heard his brother-in-law come in, and saw that Norman had only just realized what a massive gaffe he had made. "Oh it's you, is it? Well, you've heard what I said. Gates shut. Not fit to be a Master of foxhounds." Bill swallowed his drink, banged the glass on the counter, and stomped out, followed by his stony-faced wife, his family and McNeill, smirking, bringing up the rear. Norman looked at the floor. There was silence.

"If it's any consolation," said an elderly fox-hunting farmer, "he's nearly as wrong as you. He lets old Missus, tittle-tattling away, wind him up and everyone knows she's angling for a job for that up-country son-in-law. Family affairs have no place in hunting." A murmur of agreement, pleasantly tinged with self-righteousness, ran round before normal chat and banter took hold again. Norman felt that keeping family affairs out of hunting was by now a forlorn hope; he knew he really needed Jean back.

He was finishing his drink when Maria came in. He hadn't noticed she wasn't in the family party. "Hallo," said Norman. "Big row," said Maria, "or so I hear. I'm sick to death of it all. Mother nagging Dad, and plotting away, and McNeill phoning up to gossip. Mike's boring me silly; thank god we haven't got kids. I wish I could get away. I've got a friend in Truro, but I haven't got a car." Norman made up his mind. "I'm going down west on Friday. I'll give you a lift to your girlfriend in Truro's place."

After galloping on the moor with a depleted following on Thursday, Norman set off with Maria on Friday after tending to his dogs and horses.

He arrived in Newlyn late, about half-past ten, and was pleased to find the place awake, lights on in the harbour, generators running on the trawlers, a huge refrigerated truck filling up with fish straight from a deep-sea boat just in. The half-dozen pubs, small, scruffy, but friendly and lively, were still doing good business, and in the third one he found Jean, apparently waiting for the fisherman's return.

She heard him out, and came to a decision.

She scribbled a note for her friend, and left it in an envelope for him with the barmaid. On the way back, Norman told her all the details of the quarrel, his fears for his job, his standing, and his hounds and horses. When they got back, too tired to talk, they slept.

The next day was a Saturday, the day of the Harrier's meet at Trelawney's farm, so they stayed home. Jean, who always knew what to do, made sure she was near a gate she could offer to open when the hunt went past, and the Master and his son smiled and waved, because this quarrel wasn't really the Harriers' quarrel, and they didn't want to get involved, beyond a little enjoyable gossip.

That evening, Jean said to Norman, "Smarten yourself up, we're off to the Plume of Feathers, we'll find out what's what." "But what if…they'll all be in there…after the hunt…?" "New tweed jacket now! I can deal with them!" And, of course, she could.

A lot happens in a couple of days, Jean said, sometimes. "Come on, we want to get there before the crowd."

"Hallo Jean," said Len the landlord. "Glad you're back. Can't have all the women leaving." Jean, who had guessed what was possibly coming next, looked inscrutable. "Heard the news?" continued Len, "Maria's cleared out. Mike got a letter this morning. Some Canadian fancy-man down Truro, apparently." Norman's mouth was open. As he closed it prior to speaking, Jean caught his eye and shook her head. He said nothing. "Your sister's some put out!" said Len. "Ah, poor Anne! I've only just got back. I must go and see her." Neither Norman, or Len for the moment, saw the glorious irony of Jean, arch-bolter, offering comfort to her straight-laced sister for her daughter taking after her aunt.

Within the hour, Anne Trelawney, her husband, her obedient son, and her youngest daughter entered the bar. Olver glared at Norman. Jean stood up, opened her arms to her sister, "Len's told me. Come, and talk to me." Anne's face said plenty, but she wasn't impervious to her sister's charm, she was upset, and she was cautious of her sister's witty tongue. Anne did as her sister told her. Norman, for lack of anything else to do, bought Dora an orange juice. "What's new, Dora?" he asked, not sure if this was quite appropriate once he'd said it. But with the self-absorption of the very young, Dora turned and grinned, "Dad says I can go to College, do the horse course!" "A change of heart then, Olver?" ventured Norman cautiously. "Needs to broaden her horizons a bit before she settles down," growled Olver. Norman thought Olver might've had enough of horizon-broadening with Maria, but to himself luckily.

McNeill and the unwanted husband stayed away.

Bumping into Norman on the way to the WCs, out of sight and earshot of the bar, Jean chuckled. "You'll never guess! Mike gets Maria's letter this morning, then Anne caught McNeill canoodling with Dora, on a quiet bit of the hunt. Tore him off a strip, called him a dirty old man, and cancelled their shoeing contract."

"But she used to…"

"Yes, but now Maria's left, she doesn't want a hunting job any more; doesn't want Mike. She was only ever using McNeill, dafty, to undermine you."

Poor Norman. He understood these things when Jean pointed them out, but he could never work them out on his own. His instinct to get Jean back had been spot on, though, he thought. "What shall I do now?" he asked. "Nothing! Except a few meets nearer Callington. Just be pleasant to everyone, you're good at that, and say no more."

Jean was right. The quarrel vanished as though it had never been, the plotters were confounded, and Norman got to keep his Mastership, his hounds and his horses — and his wife — for the foreseeable future. What's round the corner, of course, no-one knows.

Five

The Ghost at Trevorrick Moor

Trevorrick Moor is the name of a house, at least three centuries
old, but not grand enough to be recorded anywhere. It takes its
name from the parcel of land it stands on, which had once been the
rough grazing land that went with the even older, more sheltered
farm in the combe below. Trevorrick Moor had been a small farm
for centuries, and had an old orchard, and still had a deep, deep
well, cut through the stony soil at great expense of labour, for the
river was half a mile down a steep hill. As time passed, it became
less than a farm, a smallholding, where the Pender family had to
earn wages to supplement the farm income. When this became
economically unviable, its twenty acres of land was sold to the bigger, neighbouring farmer, and the house, near derelict, was sold to
an energetic, hard-up youngish couple who turned it into a family

home again, but one with a new roof, mains electricity, and lavatories that flushed. One day it would be refurbished yet again, as a merchant banker's holiday home; but this was in the future when this story starts.

During the long slog of building work, while her husband was working elsewhere to bring in the money, the wife would mix cement for the local builder, whose skills were appropriate for the old fashioned masonry. Fernley had been born two miles away, and was full of knowledge, in a way modern city folk hardly ever are, about the lives and histories of his neighbours. Fernley believed in ghosts: the area was full of them, if you did but know. Elizabeth told him how, before they had purchased the house, one evening in late summer, with her little son and husband, she had visited Trevorrick Moor. Returning to pick up a forgotten dog lead in the dusk, Elizabeth felt a rush, out of the house, past her shoulders: like spirits leaving. She spoke of this to Fernley, for she knew Mrs. Pender had died upstairs: Mr. Pender had told her so. "But that's alright, I met her once. I'm sure she won't mind us living here," said Elizabeth. Fernley looked wry, coughed a bit. "What?" said Elizabeth. "Well, twand't Mrs. Pender. I can tell 'ee the tale, but no names: the women still live round these parts."

And so the narrative that follows unfolded.

Back when the Penders Elizabeth had known were young,

Trevorrick Moor was still a working smallholding, but Simon, who sold her family the place, and his younger brother Edward both had jobs. Mrs. Pender only had one baby then, and kept the poultry and did the garden, and of course, kept house for the men.

* * * * *

One day in high summer, the sky, before the sun came up, was luminous. On the last day of his life, Ed backed the lorry out of the lean-to at the orchard end with great care, as he always did. The air was scented still with the night's honeysuckle, and the early birdsong, just beginning, was like music. Even the tinkling of the empty churns sounded more melodious than usual. Ed wasn't really one to notice light, air, and musical sounds but this morning, he did. He took a deep breath, and admired the big beech trees beginning to glow in the light as the sun rose, and listened as the humming of millions of insects beginning the work of the day gently grew. It was Ed's daily task to collect milk churns from the farms. Back then, all sorts of tiny farms milked a few cows, and milk collection was arranged from farm gates in the metal containers one sometimes sees painted in bric-a-brac shops today.

Ed loved his job. His country upbringing meant early rising came naturally to him; as he liked to point out, you never saw animals sleeping when the sun was up, or burning electricity staying up late. Nocturnal animals he glossed over, and certainly they never use electricity. Ed felt happy with animals; it seemed to him that their habits—eat when hungry, drink when thirsty, mate when given the chance—were sensible. A lot of problems arose, he thought, when people tried to embroider, with religion or philosophy or politics, on these simple givens of mammalian life. Ed ate heartily, drank his tea, and alcohol in moderation—a hangover is no joy for anyone. As a young man, unmarried and unattached, he could see no reason why the animals' code for mating shouldn't apply as well. He liked driving his lorry, enjoyed watching the changing seasons in different parts of his area, seeing the first primroses in the moorland lanes, hearing the cuckoos in late April on the heights, seeing the crops and animals changing with the months. He would have been exasperated if anyone had complimented him on his deep familiarity with the natural and farming cycles of his part of Cornwall, and protested that most other people knew what he did—and so they may have done, then. He lived in his brother's house, that had been his father's house; he contributed to the household, and his brother's wife cooked for him and everyone else, and washed their clothes. He was grateful, but accepted it as natural, a division of work between the genders. In the same way he would expect to drive Dorothy to town if she wanted to go. He never thought of her lasciviously for she was his brother's wife. This stricture was lighter because although he loved her like a sister, he didn't fancy her at all.

One day he supposed he would move out and marry — or marry, and move out.

Ed liked meeting the people he did in the course of his driving. As is often the case, those who lived furthest from the village or hamlet, and saw less of other folk, made visitors more welcome; and he looked forward to the regular invitations to come in for a quarter of pasty or a bit of saffron cake and cup of tea. People baked at home, more, then.

Usually, farmers and their wives were on the holdings, but there was a kind of unspoken rule that men didn't enter the homes of married women unless the husbands were there. Women on their own invited men in, even for a cup of tea, at the risk of the invitation being warmly interpreted. Of course, sometimes the rules were set aside. Ed was a little contemptuous of those men — they varied from delivery van drivers to auctioneers and even vets — who sought out those women willing to bend the rules. It seemed a little unmanly, too much like the little rooster in the yard sneaking up on hens when the cockerel was elsewhere.

One of the farms where Ed collected milk was high up on the moors, down a short track. The people were Cornish, but better educated than most moorland folk. The wife had taught in a school, and the husband had engineering skills and drove off early to the docks at Falmouth to earn enough money to lift the worry of making the farm pay from their shoulders.

When, one day, Margaret asked him if he'd like a cup of tea, he wondered if, with their different backgrounds, he'd better just assume that was all it meant. He found her attractive, if quite a bit older than himself, but sat down respectful and without his usual confidence, which quite possibly improved him. She talked; she seemed a little lonely. She had had her children young, and both had left now. They didn't come home much and she missed them. He listened, then talked himself and she listened. At one point the yapping of a young dog interrupted them. "I'd tie him up when he's alone, he may get into mischief," advised Ed. "But he hates it so," Margaret replied, and Ed let it go at that. Another day, she asked him in again. Ed began to look forward to calling at Condurrow. He found himself thinking about Margaret quite a lot, but was afraid that if she could read his mind, she'd stop asking him in. He'd still never met the husband.

One day, Ed arrived at Condurrow to find Margaret weeping in the yard, inconsolable, like a little girl. The reason for her sorrow was not far to see: a young dog lay with its head half blown off by a shotgun blast. Ed found a shovel and buried the poor creature in a corner of a pasture field; he didn't really need to ask. It was the young dog he's heard yapping once or twice before. A neighbouring farmer, furious with his sheep chased more than once, had rung up early, caught the husband before work. The taciturn husband had shot the offender, stopping the yap and the complaining. This was what most people on the farms would do; but he hadn't buried the body, he hadn't cared about his wife's feelings for the animal. He had gone straight off to his job in the docks, without a word. Ed was quite shocked at the manner of the shooting, not the shooting itself. Of course, unmarried himself, he failed to think that there may have been endless arguments over the destructive pet, and that the husband, late for work, was exasperated beyond bearing by his wife's indulgence of the dog, and hated his task of execution. All Ed saw was an absent husband, cold-hearted and uncaring, and Margaret broken-hearted. He put his arms around Margaret for warmth, and she collapsed into them. The rest you can imagine.

Ed and Margaret fell in love. Ed never seriously believed there would be what is called a solution, although he sometimes fantasized about life with her if she wasn't already married. He loved her but she was married. The snatched pleasures and romance were the sweeter, and he dreamed about her. Although he would have scoffed if anyone had said so, Ed fell truly deeply for Margaret. But he didn't imagine her leaving her husband in reality, and even when, after eighteen months, she said she thought she was with child, Ed knew it would, as far as the world was concerned, be born in wedlock, and brought up by Margaret and her husband. That, as Ed would have said, was how it belonged to be.

Ed travelled to other places, besides round his moorland parishes, and the contrasts he observed fascinated him. Although happily rooted in his country world, he never minded sampling the life the towns could offer as long as he knew he could return, just as if he had never been away, to home when he wanted. About once a month, he drove a cattle lorry to Truro, for a firm in the nearest market town, and when he was away, his brother would cover the milk round for him. Because these forays brought in money over and above his regular pay, and because they took him to a larger town, out of the familiar world of his family, friends and workmates, Ed behaved in a different manner from his everyday self at home. He spent most of the money he made on himself for a start. He would eat steak and chips in a café, and used to take clothes to change into with him. The clothes were smarter, more 'town' than those he'd wear to the local at home. Nearly always he had to stay overnight—his boss would pay for a B&B—and on these occasions he'd sample what night life Truro had to offer.

It was on one of these excursions that he'd met Mandy. In a fairly innocent club, a pert and pretty girl approached him. Flattered and attracted, Ed bought her a drink. She half teased him for his rural ways, but plainly felt at ease with them. Mandy was younger than himself, and quite willing to let him pay for everything. He settled into the game; it would have its rewards. If he had had to give the game a name, he'd have called it "sugar daddy and young piece." Much of the excitement for Ed was feeling a bit of a stud, dating a young girl on the side, what others might like to do but couldn't.

Mandy and he took to meeting up on a regular basis. She would wait for him in the lounge bar of a pub. He never failed to be there dead on time on the day before the monthly cattle market; there was no need for telephone calls. Mandy had a bedsit, but he would always return to his B&B before daybreak—preventing talk, and not to miss the breakfast his boss had paid for. To Ed, this was a separate world. He was only doing what any man might do—a single man. It didn't interfere with Margaret, and of course, if he'd been able to be with her properly, he wouldn't have done it. Sometimes he felt a bit aggrieved about Margaret; he thought he really loved her, it wasn't fair. Then, he felt he didn't need to justify Mandy. But after six or so months, he rather tired of his game, and avoided going to the pub. He left a message there to say he couldn't make it, and that salved his conscience. So, it came as a shock when she caught him, cornered him he rather felt, coming out of the cattle market early in the evening on a trip two months later. He was more shocked when she'd had her say. She was tearful and furious at his neglect. Ed had always assumed he might be one of several in her life — probably had some younger chap with no money, who couldn't afford to buy her steak and wine. The idea that she went to her office job each day thinking only of him came as a shock; a worse one was news of her pregnancy. In his view girls who went up to men in nightclubs had no business getting themselves pregnant — everyone could get the pill. Was she sure he was the father? This produced such a flood of tears that Ed realized he was. He would pay for an abortion, private if necessary. He would make a journey down in a fortnight with as much money as she needed, only he hadn't a clue about how to arrange such things. She would have to do that.

Ed was quite genuine about finding the money. He found all desire for Mandy had drained away; he cursed himself. He returned home as depressed as he had ever been. In fairness to Ed, the money was the least thing worrying him. What a mistake! How foolish (and how hurtful) he had been. He didn't want to marry her, didn't want a child running around fatherless. He should have stayed near home, where he could be sure of interpreting the signals right.

The next time he saw Margaret he was quiet and glum: he could hardly talk to her about it, could he? But on his next trip to Truro, braced for a horrible time, things turned out better than he'd hoped.

When he went to the bedsit, a new tenant answered the door. Mandy had gone home, said the girl — no, she had no idea where, she had left, rent paid, no hard feelings, no-one had asked. Ed didn't know which office she had worked in, and guiltily grateful, knew that Mandy didn't know where he lived. He drove home with a lightened heart; he felt like he imagined a snared fox, suddenly loosed, would feel. Tomorrow he would see Margaret; perhaps he should think about his life and how he managed it, but not today.

Next day, when Ed arrived at Condurrow, on the day of the luminous early morning light and birdsong, Margaret rushed into the yard at the sound of his lorry, a thing she had never done before. Puzzled, he stared through the windscreen and saw to his dismay the distraught, crumpled face she had worn on the day the collie had been shot. He climbed out of the cab with a terrible feeling of misgiving.

A horrified story tumbled from her lips. It was a tale of deception and trust abused, her beloved, albeit neglectful, daughter's cruel abandonment in pregnancy by a man she had thought loved her as much as she loved him. To make things worse, he wanted her to get rid of the baby! A hard-hearted lorry driver, out for what he could get, said Margaret. Oblivious to irony in her distress, she added, the bastard's probably married. Ed's legs felt weak. Things seemed to swim before he eyes. "You can't come in today, my darling, she's here…I think she'll have to stay here too…" And glancing through the window, of course, Ed saw Mandy.

Margaret thought his distress was because he couldn't come in as he usually did, and she put her arms around him when they walked far enough away from the house. Ed buried his despairing head in her neck and hugged her; then blindly climbed into his cab and somehow drove home.

He parked the lorry in the shed that he had so happily left earlier that summer day; and his eye fell on the coil of rope in the corner and the stout 'A' frame of the rafters. He remembered his thoughts of the fox loosed from the snare yesterday. Fool again! He'd rejoiced too soon. The 'A' frame burned on his retina like an answer.

* * * * *

Mrs. Pender had heard the lorry return and wondered why Ed hadn't appeared: the midday meal was almost ready. So she walked down the track to the shed at the end of the orchard, and there made her grisly discovery of poor Ed, hanging from the beam. If Ed had thought of this, he might not had done it there and then; but he hadn't. It is to be hoped that Margaret never quite worked out what his reasons were, when she eventually heard of his suicide, but that hope may be forlorn. Over time, with shreds of information from here and there, some of it back from Truro, most people in Ed's home area worked it out, and that is why Fernley could be so sure that it was Ed's ghost, finally leaving Trevorrick Moor.

Six

Tarmac and Scrap

Sid Pooley was a farmer's son, from the poor land that lies, high up and windswept, below the moors and above the cliffs of the North Cornish coast. The farm wasn't that profitable, and there were other, older sons; as a youth Sid was wild, and over-fond of the pub. So he left the farming to his soberer brothers, and worked on the roads, drove a lorry, and learned the art of tarmac-laying.

Sid was tall and thin, wiry and strong; but it was his personality that marked him out. Possessed of a sharp intelligence, untrammeled by education, his insights were often accurate and his words well-chosen; he exerted a leader's influence over his workmates and cronies. He had never really learned to read and write, but he had mastered practical mathematics. He dealt in this and that, and always well. His fearlessness meant he was rarely beaten in a fight. Sid married when he was quite young, a girl from a village a dozen miles away. The fact she had not been known to him as a child leant her a certain romantic distance, and for a while Sid seemed to settle down; two children were born.

But Sid's way was blocked as far as career was concerned, and his restless lively intelligence had to find its interest elsewhere. He bent the law in his working life, but no-one thought the worse of him for that, as he was fiercely honest when dealing with those he knew or if his word was given. Inevitably, the annual crop of teasing girls, just out of school and in the pubs, intrigued him, and after several years of escaping the homely snares set for him in his amours he met his match.

Emily came from a local family on her mother's side: her father was long gone. She was knowing before she was wise, and her hunger for excitement obscured what her undoubted intelligence told her. In this, she and Sid, ten years her senior, were a match.

She had a scrape with a schoolteacher when she was sixteen, and this caused gossip. She had a loud reputation by the time she was nineteen, but her good humour and boldness preserved her. She wasn't pretty, but knew how to make the best of herself; and several housewives, on her small council estate, watched half with envy as Emily picked her way across the grass in her new cheap high heels towards another rendezvous in some neighbouring pub, most weekends.

"All got up like a Christmas tree, then, Em?" called out Sid when she entered the "Racehorse" one night just before the festive holiday, dressed to kill.

"Treats on the tree are for the young ones, boy, back off!" retorted Emily, quick as a flash. Sid loved a challenge.

Emily and Sid started an affair, usually conducted after pub hours in his lorry cab. Neither was really looking for love, but their natures were so akin they found it hard to ignore each other. Sometimes Emily would pronounce it "over," and look at the younger men. Sometimes Sid would recognize the practical folly of his situation, and go back to his wife, ignoring Emily for a few weeks.

Sid and Emily had drunken escapades, and fights. They were pursued by police cars suspecting drink-driving; but they got away with everything for a while. Soon the whole locality knew about them: even those who never set foot in a pub gossiped about them. Sid's wife, who had put up with a lot, found she couldn't put up with public knowledge of what she saw as her humiliation, saw a lawyer, and started to divorce Sid.

At the same time, Emily, dismayed, found herself pregnant, and declared her intention to have an abortion. This, had it been manipulative, would have been a masterstroke, for Sid, like many overtly macho men, was sentimental, and couldn't bear the idea. Emily, unusually, let him decide, and she and Sid set up home together, and in due time their son was born. He was followed by more children, two of them daughters. Contrary to local expectation, the match was a success. Both parties were so similar and so fierce, neither dared to stray, and seemingly, neither much wanted to.

They fought and made up; Emily sometimes got "teasy" with Sid pubbing when she was pregnant; but nothing came of it. Like two lions on a plain inhabited by antelope and zebra, they stayed together.

So a decade passed, and at the end of it, Sid was forty-ish, Emily thirty. Three of their four children were at school. Sid was making good money, tarmac-laying, and still scrap-dealing on the side. In the course of his work, Sid had taken under his wing a lad, Matt, who was the son of a girl Sid had known during his brief attendances at school. Matt's father was a gipsy, and Matt had been reared in a big shiny caravan with ornate frosted windows and two Alsatian dogs. Matt learned the tarmac-laying trade, and worked alongside, and for, Sid. He and Sid got on well, very well, much as if they were of an age — which of course they weren't, Sid was Matt's parents' contemporary. Matt's attitude to Sid was always tinged with deference, almost hero-worship, which of course helped the relationship flourish. If a difference arose that had importance for Sid, Matt would give way.

Matt was a good-looking young man, fit and strong, not too bright, fond of his beer. He was a younger Sid in some ways, but not so sharp. He admired everything about Sid, and inevitably, this included Emily. Despite her child-bearing, Emily had kept her figure; she was exactly half-between Matt and Sid in age, but no-one had thought of this as yet. But Matt's deference, and admiration for Sid, acted like a brake; he never realized how attractive he found Emily. If Sid noticed, he complacently regarded it as a compliment to himself, his choice and keeping of such a woman. "Pick your jaw up off the floor, boy!" Sid would say to Matt when Emily appeared on holidays in full get-up: he was secretly pleased at the impression she could create. Of course Emily noticed, but for years now she had treated the attentions of other men as a foil for her attachment to Sid; at worst, as a mild threat, to keep him in line.

Then, the accident occurred. Sid and Matt had always been accustomed to deal in scrap when the opportunity presented itself: anything from old, Victorian cast iron mangles to wrecked cars. Indeed, the mangles, horse-drawn hay rakes and milk churns were worth more as bric-a-brac or collectables than scrap nowadays. Sid, with his usual perspicacity, had realized this well before his fellows and done well out of the trade. But unhappily this day it was wrecked cars they were coping with. One Thursday in March things seemed no different than usual. The two of them were loading five derelict cars on the back of the truck, using the old crane mounted on the vehicle. It wasn't quite up to the job anymore, but had always managed, so far, to hoist the second level cars high enough. This day, it jammed: swearing at it, Sid stepped forward to hit it with a hammer and something broke. The half-raised car fell, taking Sid with it. After the sickening thud, Matt heard Sid curse, thought, Christ, he's alive at least. Where was a phone?

The day that followed was taken up in the furore that comes after a serious accident, once the initial shock cleared. Sid was flown in a helicopter to Truro to hospital, the police arrived, Emily was informed. The days that followed that day were taken up with hospital visits, health and safety inspections, too-late warnings of dangers inherent in nearly all Sid's procedures. Sid and Matt were both self-employed, and Sid was in bigger trouble than any official could devise, so he wasn't pursued. But legal proceedings were the least of Sid's worries. For, over the days of cautious testing and waiting, it became clear that Sid had damaged his spine. As time went on, it became plain that he would not regain the lost control of his body below the waist.

Life in a wheelchair looked, not only likely, but unavoidable.

This was a predicament undreamed of by any of the three. Sid had scoffed at brushes with death, like a bravado in a film, if more cautious friends admonished him for risk-taking...but disablement, while still fully alert in the mind, while still young...he had never thought that far.

Emily's fierce loyalty sustained her for many months. She got busy, made applications for grants, explored therapies, and made her intention of building an extension for Sid on the house and keeping him at home clear to everyone: in short, she nailed her colours to Sid's mast.

Matt, loyal as a Labrador, worked on with the help of an unskilled hired lad, splitting the tarmac-laying profits with Sid with no thought for his own future. Work for tarmac-layers rarely runs out.

The extension was slowly built and fitted out. Sid grimly oversaw the work, and eventually grew strong enough to push himself around in his wheelchair for hours, and up to the "Racehorse." Home was downhill. Matt called round most evenings to report on the day's progress at work. Leaving Emily and Sid's eldest, who by now was old enough, in charge of his siblings, the three of them would go to the pub. Strangely, Sid commanded much the same measure of respect from his wheelchair amongst the local men as he had when on his feet. Matt remained deferential, Emily faithful but cautious.

It was Sid's ferocious will, that refused to recognize his disability, and the fact that it almost certainly would not be cured, that kept everyone in thrall. They too behaved as if it was a temporary set-back, and they believed all would be well, Sid back on his feet again, soon. But reality seeped round the edges of the picture Sid's will had drawn, and like damp on a watercolour, began to compromise it. Sid became grimmer, and his flashes of humour rarer, but he persevered. His burden, physical and mental, was heavy, and he found that, despite the fact (as he put it himself) that he was sitting down all day, he tired easily. Emily, practical and unfussy, coped easily enough with the extra work his condition gave her, and never hinted at dissatisfaction with any other area of her life. For this, Sid was silently grateful, and gratitude was a feeling he wasn't used to. Inevitably, one night, Sid, tired out, retired to bed early, and Matt and Emily stayed up, on their return from the pub.

Matt stayed on. This became a regular occurrence. Matt and Emily fell in love. To begin with, there was no gossip. Everyone was used to seeing Matt's van outside Sid and Emily's. Sid and Emily had almost exhausted the village appetite for tittle-tattle themselves in their youth; even the most prurient pub gossips were slow to rouse themselves over Matt. There was both fear and sympathy for Sid, and respect for her staunchness and sympathy for Emily, that, even when realization came, bridled the tongues for a while. No-one was sure if Sid knew what was going on: certainly, no-one wanted to be the one responsible for him finding out if he didn't know. But eventually the signs of a scandalous ménage a trois, deliciously shocking, became too obvious to ignore — and of course some did truly find it distasteful and wrong.

It was Norman Olver's funeral that acted as a turning point. One of several brothers who farmed on the moor, he had been a local character for years, and was well liked. Huge funerals are common in Cornish rural areas, and nearly everyone went. Sid hated funerals, and the church on its mound was inaccessible to his wheelchair, so Emily went with Matt.

Emily misjudged her outfit. Her black dress was too tight for a burial service, her shoes too high and strappy, her tights too fine: it was as if her clothes caused their own outrage, and made it impossible for folk to go on pretending they didn't realize who filled her bed now. Emily hung on oblivious Matt's loving arm, incandescent with happy gratification. A silent ripple of distaste ran through the congregation.

Nothing happened for a while.

About a month later, at a dance in the village hall, an incident occurred that sparked disaster, at least for Matt in love. At the dance were David Giles, a homely, inoffensive farmer, and his wife Hazel. They were fond of ballroom dancing, and not bad at it either. As the evening wore on, the bar at one end was taking money, Sid was drinking in his wheelchair near it with his pals. The atmosphere loosened as more beer was drunk, the elderly and prim left, the younger folk got noisier. At the little band's whim, a waltz was played and David and Hazel swung, quite gracefully, onto the floor. Emily, oblivious to the change in tempo, was hanging round Matt's neck in a nightclub clinch, and quite accidentally, David brushed her backside as he passed. Matt, who had had too much to drink, turned on Dave and grabbed him. All his confused loyalty to Sid, his undoubted love for Emily, and guilt at his cheating position as the backdoor lover of his friend's wife, found a target in poor harmless farmer David. Matt shouted, held him, smacked his jaw with his fist, and headbutted him as he fell. All this was done in front of a dozen witnesses or more. Hazel screamed, David groaned and passed out. There was silence — the band had stopped playing — for a long quarter minute. Then a man's voice in the crown muttered, "Bloody thieving gipsy, steal a man's wife." "And *she's* a bloody hypocrite!" shrieked Hazel. Sid at the bar had been oblivious of events when this commenced: now the wheelchair cut furiously through the crowd. In the old days, even at this stage, Sid could have sorted things out: smacked Matt, sent Emily home, calmed the crowd down, and even pacified Hazel. But he couldn't now. The look in his eye was terrible. "Emily, we're going home," was all he said. Emily flinched as if he'd hit her, grabbed the handles of the wheelchair, and walked out there and then, pushing while Sid propelled.

The police and an ambulance were called; David's injuries were quite serious, the attack unprovoked, and people's feelings running high. A collective feeling of despair found a scapegoat in poor Matt. Everyone sympathized with Sid; yet what was his young wife to do? Celibacy at thirty-two for a woman like Emily was as much a sentence as gaol. And she did everything for Sid. The easiest one to blame was Matt: young, fit and not known to them all from birth, a gipsy's son. Witnesses, who would normally have kept quiet, told the police what they had seen. The upshot of it all was a court appearance for Matt, and a spell in Exeter gaol. The love affair was over. When Matt came out after a few months, he didn't return; he joined a gang of travelling tarmac layers, and moved on with them.

Emily and Sid stayed together. They became grimmer, and were treated with caution, like ageing lions who could still be dangerous. Eventually, of course, time changed things: they mellowed as they grew older. The eldest girl was married, given away by Sid in his wheelchair, in top hat and tails. People never mentioned Matt the gipsy, and thought about him less and less.

The day came when the elderly labourer who was always in the pub, angling for a free beer from visitors who liked his Cornish colourfulness, took to telling a romantic story. To those who would buy him a pint, he would rehearse a version of a local near-tragedy, carefully omitting real names. Those locals who overheard him knew he was telling of beautiful Emily, devoted to crippled Sid, and the gipsy who tried to steal her away.

Seven

The China Dog

The china dog had sat above the little fireplace in Mary Nicholl's bungalow ever since Sarah had known her. It was, properly speaking, not china at all, but pottery — Staffordshire, and the survivor of a pair. Sarah thought of it as the china dog because Mary had been in the habit of glancing at it and saying, "Ole china dog! Don't 'ee look at me!" Mary Nicholl had lived in the bungalow for ten years, and had been widowed there, but it wasn't her 'real' home. It was a retirement home, bought for that purpose when the ancient old house out on the moor with its land was sold. The sale was reluctant, undertaken only when Sam her husband really became too frail to work on the moorland farm any longer. He had kept a few ducks, and reared a few bullocks annually, in the field behind his bungalow, and when he could no longer do that, he felt it was time to die. Mary missed him, but she understood why he had (literally) given up his ghost. She had expected a spell of widowhood, for she was quite a few years younger than Sam.

Sarah and her husband had bought a granite house nearby, and were renovating it. Like many older Cornish people, Mary was a valuable mine of information about the minutiae of old-fashioned farmhouse life, the purpose of artifacts and storage rooms, trivets, cloam ovens, and salting troughs, and quite happy to tell Sarah how "things belonged to be." Sarah in turn conveyed the tips and explanations to her husband, who was glad to hear them. The two women, despite the difference in their ages and backgrounds, were friends. Work on the house progressed and was almost complete when Mary followed Sam into the graveyard. She died in the spring, and there was the usual, enormous farming funeral in the local church, flowers everywhere inside in vases, and outside in the banks and hedges, and the trees coming into leaf with the sun shining through. At the funeral, Sarah met an even older woman, who turned out to be Mary's sister—her older sister Agnes.

After an interval, the bungalow was sold. Mary and Sam's two daughters had married and moved away, and the place wasn't an old family home. That was gone. At the sale of unwanted items and furniture Sarah made up her mind to buy a memento, something for the farmhouse they were doing up. The Staffordshire spaniel had always appealed to her, with its rather lugubrious stare. The fact there was only one meant it wasn't worth much to dealers, but several people took a fancy to it, and Sarah paid more for it than she'd intended.

At the sale, Sarah saw Mary's sister Agnes again. Family members would have taken what keepsakes they wanted before the sale; it was probably just curiosity that brought Agnes there. Agnes came up to Sarah after the little auction, looking amused, and said, "You got the 'ole china dog then — did Mary tell 'ee how she came by it?" "No," said Sarah, "she used to say it was looking at her. She said she'd tell me someday, but she never quite found the time." "Well, see. It reminded her of something she didn't want to forget, but something she knew she hadn't managed right," said Agnes. And, as they walked down the road in a companionable way, Agnes told Sarah what Mary (God rest her) had never got round to telling.

When Agnes and Mary were young, out on the moor on the farm their grandfather had farmed and their father inherited, with their sister and brother, life had been in an archaic world, twice removed from the present day. Everyone farmed, or was married to a farmer. Everyone worked from dawn to dusk, and by lantern light, and thought nothing of it. Dairy pasture and garden, barley field and hay meadow prospered under their patient nursing, where today only rough grass, gorse and bracken are to be seen. Between

73

the old stone walls, where today black bullocks graze, kept as much for subsidy as meat, there were once calves, sheep, dairy cows, working ponies, and poultry. The families that looked after, and lived off them, peopled the landscape. Agnes and Mary and their siblings, like all the farm children, walked miles each day, to school and back, but only after the girls had milked and done the chickens and ducks, and Wilfrid had fed the cattle and the pigs. All the cash the household had was from selling butter and eggs to a man and cart that called round in summer to collect them, and from calves and a pig or two sold for further fattening to the richer, lower-lying farmers. A pig or two were killed and salted down for household use; those enormous granite troughs, cut from a single piece of stone, were for that. No-one employed labourers on a moorland farm like Mary's Darras - low as the wages were, they could not be afforded.

Agnes interrupted her story. "Me and Mary once went up to the gate and wept to see the state the place is in now." She shed a tear or two telling Sarah as she walked. "It was our home all through our girlhood and I can't help it. Our brother Wilfrid doesn't take it the same way. He says, 'giddome, maid, you must think no-one could say it wasn't farmed proper when you lived there.' It's true. There were twenty gates, and you could put any animal into any field, and it would stay there, the hedges was so well kept. We

74

scrubbed the granite yard once a week, my sisters and me." Agnes wiped her eyes and continued with her tale.

In this world, full of sky and weather, animals being born and killed, unremitting work, but freedom from timesheet and factory, there was a cast of human players that hardly altered, unless by death or birth. Daily, people like Agnes and Mary saw and worked with their families; they met the children of the neighbouring farms at school; they saw the whole — or the respectable, larger part — of their world at Chapel, on a Sunday. Inevitably, girls were accorded less freedom than boys. Although the girls would see animals born and suckled as soon as they could walk, and be familiar with the mechanics of animal matings, chastity and modesty were virtues no young girl could afford to be without. Agnes and Mary had never been further than Bodmin, and then with their mother, or on a Sunday School 'treat' — an annual picnic outing in a large wagonette, hired for the occasion by the worthies of the Chapel.

Mary, said Agnes, was an exceptionally pretty girl. She didn't realize it, for she had no-one to compare herself to, and only one old, spotted mirror in the house, in mother and father's bedroom — vanity was a terrible failing. Mary was small, and delicately made for one so strong. She had that happy colouring seen sometimes in the far west, blue eyes and near-black, long curly hair. And her face was pretty, her skin and teeth perfect. (Agnes was a bit jealous, but loved her sister, and sensibly, concentrated on her own love life and married the son of a neighbouring farmer when she was twenty-three, and Mary eighteen.) Mary was a vivacious, uncomplicated girl. If she had a fault, it was what her family called being hoity-toity. If put out, or offended by something, she would put her nose in the air and flounce a little, and then find a job that needed doing—others had to guess what it was that was wrong, she would never tell. Sometimes no-one tumbled to the cause, life trundled on, until everyone, including Mary, forgot about it.

When Mary was eighteen, there was a new arrival in the parish. On one of the biggest farms, that had south facing land more fertile than most, the Pencrebers took on a farm-servant, as labourers were called. He was a lad from off the moor, whose farming parents had died. Only nineteen, he was forced to use his only skills to keep himself, and lived-in with his employers, eating with them and going to Chapel with them on Sundays. Tragedy had struck him out of the blue, wiping out his emotional and material security in one fell swoop, when both his parents were killed in an accident. He was an only child and the farm was rented. This had made him older than his nineteen years in some ways; he had learned that broken-hearted, one survives, and that nothing, however dear, can be taken for granted. Because knowledge of his background was sketchy (compared to those who had been born in the parish) folk kept a wary eye on him at first. He was a fine-looking lad, with manners and a good nature, and after six months of hard work and good behaviour through the summer months on his part, the general opinion formed, that it was safe to let him over the threshold. If a few young female hearts beat faster at the idea of a more open season, it was in vain. For young Joshua (that was the orphan's name) and Mary had fallen in love months ago.

In the only times they could see each other — Chapel — enough glances had been exchanged for the two of them to know, in their untested hearts, that each was besotted with the other. In that world, with no images of pop or film stars, no aids to beauty or manliness, just the luck of birth, exercise and fresh air, among a population that scarcely changed, true physical attraction, when it struck, must have been like a thunderbolt, especially for the young, experiencing it for the first, maybe the only, time. Marriages founded on it could last a happy lifetime, and so perhaps it would be in this case. Very gradually, the romance progressed. The delicious thrill that Mary and Joshua felt will have to be imagined when, one day, their fledgling romance was recognized. After several months of only just daring to address each other directly by name to say, hello, goodbye, they were allowed to walk the hundred yards from Chapel to Mary's family's pony and jingle, unaccompanied by an eavesdropping younger sister or her parents—although the latter were not far behind.

Joshua and Mary were walking out, as it was called. They were nineteen and eighteen years respectively: it would be an age before they could marry, they thought. They had no home of their own, and no real income, but love thrived. They walked the moorland paths through autumn and winter, hastening to finish their myriad tasks before they could meet. Never had the red-flushed blackberry leaves and the tawny bracken looked so beautiful to either of them. When autumn turned to winter, what they would remember was the magic of the moor under its rare snowfalls, when the sky was pewter grey and the ground glistened white, and the streams froze, not the increased load of work feeding cattle and sheep hungry in the cold, and the worry of whether the hay supply would hold out till first growth in April. When spring came, happily before the animals had gone no more than a little hungry, the burgeoning seemed to be, for Josh and Mary, specially for them. The lovers were caught in a sort of dreamy egotism, where the apple trees blossom, the bees work, the lambs leap, just to celebrate their finding of each other. Another year passed, almost as magical as the first.

Joshua turned twenty-one, Mary twenty. Josh began to think of maybe finding a job that had a cottage. His employer, who did not want to lose him, began to consider whether a ruinous one-up, one-down cottage could be repaired with stone and slate to hand. Apart from Josh's value on the farm, he and his wife were fond of the lad, and in a sense this led to an unwanted outcome. Usually the farmer took his son with him to the summer fair in the richer lands to the south at Liskeard. It was a two-day trip, driving the animals, too far for the pony there and back in one day. This year, as a mark of Joshua's now-accepted status as a man courting, a trusted employee growing up, he took him as well. They were going to the area where Josh's parents had farmed. He wanted to go, but was wary of how he would feel, seeing the old familiar scenes again. Before he went, Mary flounced a little and went home early once or twice. If her sisters had been there, they would have teased her about 'going hoity-toity.' Not knowing what they did, Josh was upset. He grimly remembered how things had changed, once before.

Mary had never been to a fair. For well-brought up, Chapel girls from moor farms there was still a dangerous, illicit side to fairs in the mind. Preachers made fierce imprecations against the sort of vices — drink and worse — that fairs might lead to. In the mining districts farther west the great fairs had been famous for drunken revelry, rioting and mayhem within grandparents' memory. Mary's imagination kindled at the idea of the fair and its dangerous temptations. So at the end of June, Josh was going to the fair, pleased to be asked but nervous of the emotions returning south might bring;

Mary was suddenly insecure, aware there might be attractions in the wide world she could only imagine.

Josh went to the fair. He felt a lump in his throat when he saw the familiar hills on the horizon, but it wasn't uncontrollable. He thought of Mary lovingly. Absence makes the heart grow fonder, and distance diminishes the perception of difficulty.

Josh saw very little of the fleshpots of temptation. The worthy farmer didn't even go near the area where the doubtful spirits sold and the tarts' booths were discreetly set up. They drank a few half pints of beer, and had a go at a coconut shy. There was a rifle range with airguns deliberately skewed, but nice prizes. Josh noted his gun and returned next day, and with the same gun, much to his own and the stallholder's surprise, won a pair of Staffordshire spaniels. A handsome prize: he was very proud of it. He packed the dogs in hay in a box, and they travelled home safely. Mrs. Pencreber approved, but they weren't for her. Next day he set off for Darras. Now Mary had been slowly simmering for three days during the absence of her intended. Not that she suspected him of drunkenness or fornication—both cost a lot of money, for a start—but because she felt left out. Mary had gone from hoity-toity to a passion of resentment. When Josh arrived, she wouldn't let him take her hand, wouldn't kiss him—and worst of all, she wouldn't tell him what was wrong. This was because she couldn't put anything into words; all those times in her childhood when she had one of her fits of temper, she had never had to explain herself, and now she could not. Josh went home, and stayed away for a couple of days. When he went back, again with the china dogs, it was worse. When he tried to give her the present, she stuck her nose in the air. "What makes 'ee think I'll want the filthy fairings?" she rudely said. With a face like thunder, Joshua threw the spaniels on the ground and turned and walked away. One of them broke. Coming into the yard from the milking shed, Agnes, unaware, assuming an accidental breakage, said, "What a shame!" "You keep it then!" sparked Mary, crying. She was beginning to lose heat, and to regret her moody harshness.

It would be hard to say who was the most upset by the day's disastrous events. Mary had brought it on herself, but that was no consolation. She did what she had done as a child, toiled tirelessly at as many tasks as she could find to do, as if seeking expiation through hard work. Josh was hurt and angry, but felt himself not to blame; it was impossible for him to see inside Mary's mind, so he looked for reasons elsewhere. Had she had second thoughts? Had someone else started to replace him in her affections? Josh didn't want to break his heart again. The pain of losing his parents, especially his mother, was still with him. Something in him froze, and he stayed away from Darras. Days, a week went by, and every time he thought of Mary, he thought he felt the beginning of the pain he remembered from the days after the accident that had lost him his parents.

A few months later they heard he'd left the Pencrebers' farm, and gone away to work on the rich land down south of Liskeard. He never did come back to Darras. One day in the future he would get his own farm, and marry, and his son's son would become a leading organic meat supplier, making money in a good way — but this was all undreamed of, in the future. Now, there were just two miserable young people. But youth can heal, and after some months Mary's unhappiness began to ease.

She stayed on the farm, and five years later married Sam, who was good and honest, plain and honourable and thirteen years older than her. When Sam's father died, they took over his farm, and the girls were born. Wilfrid took over Darras, but moved off the moor before Sam retired. A year after she married, Mary asked her sister for the ''ole china dog'. Agnes of course gave it to her. Mary was happy enough with Sam; she had never known what living with Josh might have been. But she never felt that high exhilaration, that excitement in everything from the morning sun to the owl's hoot, that she had felt every day for a year when she and Josh were courting. Although perhaps latterly dimly-remembered, the china dog was a link for her to a more intense living.

By now Sarah and Agnes had reached Sarah's home, and drunk

a cup of tea. Sarah's husband had come in and heard the last part of the story. He had been a bit taken aback at the price of one half of a pair of Staffordshire dogs. "She was jealous, see," continued Agnes. "She'd always been the prettiest and the liveliest in our little world, but she'd never been further than Bodmin, never to a 'do' apart from Chapel things, never read anything but schoolbooks or the bible, and she was jealous when her young man took just one step in to the big wide world outside. You never know, she was probably better off with Sam, but you could say her tantrum cost her her lover."

"Ah!" said Sarah's husband laughing. "I see now why the china dog was worth so much."

Eight

Leskernick

The grey, granite house had probably stood out on the moor, too far out for company or comfort, for about a hundred and seventy years. It had its back to the west, and had a grim, determined look, even on a sunny day when the skylarks were singing. To get to it, you left the tarmac road in the hamlet a few miles away, drove down a track past other old farms, and over a rough ford in a little river bottom, idyllic on warm summer days with damsel flies. The way then led up through boulders and gorse onto open moor rising steep up ahead, and on again. The little farmhouse had been built by tenant farmers on a three-lives lease, when people expected to work hard all day every day on the land just to keep themselves and the family, and its reason for being had gone.

Once there must have been children there, a dog in the yard, a cat or two, bantams and muscovy ducks, cattle, a pig, and at least one pony for transport. Someone had planted beech trees, on the bank enclosing the garden behind the house, for shelter, and most had survived, albeit stunted by the gales. The granite slabs, called in Cornwall a coffin stile, set in the gateway to protect vegetables from cattle, still remained. Regardless of this defence, the near constant scour of the wind had sanded away all the homely plants that had once grown there, and now the sour turf ran right up to the walls with just a few hawthorns that blossomed in the early summer. Older people in the hamlet on the highroad could remember two old women, sisters, the last of the last family to farm, living there long after farming ceased, with oil lamps and well, turf and gorse for fuel; they lived on for years on the unexpected luxury, for them, of a state pension.

Their strategy for emergency had a magnificent simplicity: if they ever really needed help, it was agreed that they would hang a large white sheet from a bedroom window, a signal visible to the roadside hamlet a few miles away. This was resorted to when one of them died there; she was sadly followed, not long after, by the other. The house fell into slow dereliction, but it was strongly built and resisted decay; eventually the local estate owners' representative put it to auction, and it was sold.

Max, the man who bought it and owned it and enjoyed it for

many years, was an unlikely match for the house at first sight. He was a lawyer, with a practice near London, of middle European descent.

But he knew what he wanted, and when it was realized what that was, local people accepted it with relief. He had the house repaired where it needed it, in a plain traditional fashion, and made fast against the weather. He installed a small generator in a shed, that lit the house and ran a pump in the well, and that was it. He had an old green landrover that would go over anything, and didn't need a track. He usually came on his own, but sometimes brought his wife with him in summer, and sometimes stayed as long as a fortnight, bothering no-one, apparently soaking up the solitude, the sky and the weather. He watched birds, and foxes, and the occasional red deer that crossed the moor, moving from the scrub-filled valleys of the north to the cornfields on the south.

Rough-coated half-wild subsidy cattle were his neighbours, and he waved and shouted a greeting to their owners when they passed his house occasionally on horseback or in a landrover. He paid for all his locally-purchased needs cheerfully on time, and passed the time of day with those he met in affable fashion, and so he was well enough liked. This went on for a decade or more, and the lawyer, and the landrover kept in a garage in the nearest town for its purpose, grew older but kept going.

But the world changed, as it always does, and one day those changes made themselves felt, even at Leskernick.

No-one found out who the culprits were: there was a small gallery of types, none local, to choose from. Years ago, and miles away on the same moor, a small fascist group had tried training survivalists in a similar remote kind of property. The Territorials regularly came to the moor and "played silly buggers," as the older locals cynically described the training exercises, and even Naval attachments held orienteering sessions there, to the disgust of the cattlemen. Where was the sense in that? Where was the sea? Certainly the last two weren't suspected: it was always possible there were criminals, on the run from somewhere. Hippies were unlikely, because of the nature of the crime. It was probably criminals on the run.

What happened was this: one November Max turned up, as was his habit, out of the blue, in his landrover, after dark, to find his house broken into. There was no vehicle he saw, and the generator wasn't running, or he would have been alerted: but inside were two or three men, with a candle or two lit, eating and smoking. Max wouldn't have stayed out at Leskernick if he had been a nervous man; he was bold, and now he was furious as well. As he started in, with "What the hell is…," he was socked on the head, and passed out.

He came to, hours later, and found himself very efficiently bound to a chair and gagged, tied so strongly that he could not wriggle across the floor even when he managed to fall over, banging his head again. The men had gone; it was still dark, beginning to lighten in the east. Slowly, the seriousness of his predicament dawned on him. His attackers could not have known, but no-one would miss his landrover from its lock-up in Liskeard, and his wife was used to not hearing from him for up to a fortnight. The hamlet couldn't see his vehicle from so far away, and if they could it wouldn't mean anything had gone wrong. Max struggled and tried to stretch this way and that, but he could not get free.

Up early on his farm at Wheal Fortune, Jack Dennis whistled his dog as he prepared to drive out on the moor with bales of hay for the cattle on the down. Looking around for the collie, his eye caught Leskernick as a watery ray of sunshine illuminated its front, and he saw a white sheet hanging: he looked again, and it *was* a sheet, still there when the sun faded. He could swear to it; then he remembered the tale of the sisters, and their emergency plan, from his boyhood, and his dog suddenly appeared. Puzzled, wondering, he came to a decision. "We'll go the long way round, Moss," he said to the dog, and set off. In the dip, the track loses sight of the old farmhouse, on the way out, and it takes a while to get there. When Jack drove over the rise and saw the house, the sheet had gone. He was glad he hadn't made himself the butt of possible jokes by telling anyone yet what he'd seen; but now he was here, he'd have a closer look, and just keep quiet if nothing was wrong.

Max had heard the landrover, and was making as much noise as he could, a ghastly gurgling through the gag. He heard the engine stop, and footsteps on the ground outside. Jack saw the broken window pane just as he heard Max's strangulated cries.

And so a tragedy was averted. No sheet was hanging, or blowing about in the yard. The police came, and found no more than obvious evidence of the truth of Max's story. Max wasn't injured, and decided it hadn't put him off: he just needed more secure locks. Jack Dennis was a local celebrity for quite a few weeks, and quite relished telling his story, and how certain he was about the sheet, now events had turned out the way they had. Max added to the mystery by saying he had no such sheets at Leskernick. What to think?

Tom the old potboy up at the pub had the last word, as he often did, if only because he talked more than most. According to Tom, it was the *house* that did it, see: the house was haunted, and the sisters had always said that a sheet would hang out the window in a *real* emergency. He would nod, then, satisfied with his explanation, and go back to work. This time, he deserves the last word, for no-one else has a better explanation.

ISBN 141209516-6